Personal copy - O. Norgord

Text copyright © 1988 Justin Knowles Ltd
Illustrations copyright © 1988 Gill Sampson
Designed and Art Directed by Susan Mann
Story adaptation by Neil and Ting Morris

Published in 1988 by Ideals Publishing Corporation
P.O. Box 148000, Nashville, Tennessee 37214-8000.
Printed and bound in Italy

Produced by the Justin Knowles Publishing Group
9 Colleton Crescent, Exeter, Devon, England

ISBN 0-8249-8261-4

Peter Pan

Illustrated by Gill Sampson   Retold by Neil and Ting Morris

Designed and Art Directed by Susan Mann

CHILDREN'S CLASSICS

IDEALS CHILDREN'S BOOKS
Ideals Publishing Corporation, Nashville, Tennessee 37214

*A*ll children, except one, grow up. The exception was Peter Pan,
a magical boy whose home was Neverland.
At night he and the little fairy Tinker Bell
often flew to the big city to listen to bedtime stories.
He liked the Darlings' house best,
because Wendy knew the most exciting stories,
and he was just as good a listener as her young brothers,
John and Michael. Neverland was, of course, a make-believe island,
but it was quite real to the children.
"Peter Pan comes in through the window at night,
and sits at the end of my bed, playing a tune on his pipe,"
Wendy told her mother.

"Nonsense," Mrs. Darling replied. "You must have been dreaming, Wendy!" But that very night, Peter appeared again, and this time he left his shadow behind. Wendy put it away in a drawer and fell asleep waiting for him to come back. It was Tinker Bell who guessed where it was. But Peter couldn't stick the shadow

back on, and began to cry. This soon woke Wendy.
"The best thing is to sew it back on," she said,
getting out a needle and thread. Peter was so pleased
that he invited Wendy and her brothers to come with him to Neverland.
But first they had to learn to fly!

Peter showed them what to do, and blew some fairy dust
on each one of them. Then they flew out of the window
and high up into the night sky. "Second to the right
and straight on till morning, that's the way to Neverland,"
Peter told Wendy. It was a long journey, but at last
the children saw the island with the mermaids' lagoon
and the Indian camp. They recognized it at once,

because they had so often pretended to be there, and shuddered
when they saw the pirates' ship. "Captain Hook wants his revenge,"
warned Peter, "ever since I cut off his hand in a fight.
If they see Tink's light, they will attack!" Wendy quickly
put the fairy into John's hat, but suddenly
there was a tremendous bang. The pirates had fired!

W endy found herself alone, and was glad to hear
Tinker Bell's fairy tinkle. "It must mean 'follow me',"
she thought. But it really meant "I hate you,"
because the fairy was jealous of Wendy and wanted to teach her
a lesson. She flew with her to the hollow trees where Peter's gang,
the lost boys, lived. They were all there – Tootles,
Nibs, Slightly, Curly and the twins. Pointing at Wendy,
Tinker Bell cried, "Peter commands you to shoot Wendy,
quick, quick!" The boys always obeyed Peter's orders,
so Tootles took up his bow and arrow and shot.
Wendy was terrified, and plunged straight to the ground.
"Peter will be so pleased with me," Tootles said proudly.

*P*eter was horrified when he saw Wendy, but fortunately
she was still alive. He told the lost boys
to build a little house around Wendy for her to rest in,
and they started straight away. When at last it was finished
and Wendy came out, they asked, "Please will you be our mother
and tell us stories?" "But I'm only a little girl," laughed Wendy.
Peter didn't think that mattered, and so Wendy agreed.
"Go in at once, you naughty children," she called,
"it will soon be your bedtime." The boys rushed
straight to their underground home, and Wendy tucked
them all up in bed. Then she told them a story
and Peter played a tune.
Michael pretended to be a baby and slept in a basket.

*E*very day there were thrilling adventures with wild animals, Indians and pirates. Of course, Peter always won the fights. But one of the most exciting adventures took place at the mermaids' lagoon. Peter and Wendy often went there for a swim. Wendy enjoyed watching the mermaids comb

their long hair. Unfortunately the mermaids were not interested in her, and often splashed her with their tails.
One day when they were lazing about on the rocks, there was a sound of muffled oars. Peter, who could sense danger even in his sleep, cried, "Pirates! Hide!"
From their hiding place behind a rock they saw two pirates and their captive, Tiger Lily, the Indian princess.

Peter quickly thought up a plan. He imitated Hook's voice
and called, "Ahoy there!" The pirates thought
it was their captain and shouted back,
"We are just taking the redskin out to drown." But to their surprise,
they heard him say, "Cut the ropes and set her free."
Being obedient pirates, they did as they were ordered.
Suddenly the real Hook turned up, and he was furious
when he realized that once again he had been fooled by Peter Pan.
He tried to pull himself up the rock with his hook,
and Peter could easily have finished him off.
But thinking that it was unfair to fight from a better position,
he helped the pirate up. It was then that Hook clawed him.
But the fight was cut short when the crocodile
who was always after the captain swam up and chased him away.

The water was rising all the time, but Peter was too weak
to do anything. He told Wendy that she must leave the rock
before they both drowned. "But why can't we swim
or fly back together?" Wendy asked. "Hook wounded me,"
Peter said, "and I can neither swim nor fly." "I won't leave you,"

Wendy told him. Just then a kite flew by. Peter caught it,
tied the tail round Wendy and sent her to safety.
"To die will be an awfully big adventure," Peter thought,
when he saw the Neverbird coming to his rescue.
She lent him her nest, and he floated safely to shore.

*O*ne evening Wendy told the lost boys a very special
bedtime story. It was about Mr. and Mrs. Darling
and their three children who flew away, and the window
that was always kept open for their return.
Peter thought it was a boring story. "Long ago when I flew
back to my mother," he said, "the window was barred
and there was another little boy sleeping in my bed."

At that Michael began to cry for his own mother.
"We'll leave for home at once," said Wendy. "Can we come too?"
asked the lost boys. "Who wants to grow up?" Peter sneered,
as he watched them leave. But they walked
straight into the clutches of the pirates. Hook counted
his victims – eight boys and Wendy.
The pirates took the children to their ship and chained them up.

"You'll all walk the plank!" Hook snarled.
But Tinker Bell slipped away and alerted Peter.
Quietly he climbed aboard,
unchained the boys and cut Wendy free. Suddenly Captain Hook
was face to face with Peter Pan.

The others formed a ring around them. For a long time
the two just stared at each other. "So, Pan," said Hook,
"this is all your doing." "Aye, Hook, it is," answered Peter.
Hook drew his sword. "Well then, prepare to meet your doom,"
he growled. The great fight started.

*P*eter was much too quick and clever for Hook. "You're mine!"
Peter cried at last. Seeing Peter with his dagger poised,
Hook jumped into the sea, where the crocodile was waiting for him.
That night Wendy put the boys to bed in the pirates' bunks,
and in the morning they set sail for the Darlings' home.
The children all dressed up as pirates, Peter was captain,
and Tinker Bell came too. They flew the last part of the journey,
and when they got to the city, Wendy and her brothers
soon spotted their house.
The window was open and they flew straight in.

When Mrs. Darling went into the nursery
and saw her three children tucked up in their beds,
she was overjoyed. The lost boys were waiting downstairs,
and Mrs. Darling said at once that they could stay.
They were delighted, and all hoped that Peter would stay too.
But Peter said that his home was Neverland:
he didn't want to go to school, grow up into a man
and be sent to an office. So he and Tinker Bell flew off together.
quite happily. As Wendy waved goodbye, she knew
that she would never forget her adventures with Peter Pan.